Let's Be Friends Again!

Let's Be Friends Again!

By HANS WILHELM

SCHOLASTIC INC.
New York Toronto London Auckland Sydney

To Henning

ISBN 0-590-44802-1

12 11 10 9 8 7 6 5 4 3 2   1 2 3 4 5 6/9

Printed in the U.S.A.   08

First Scholastic printing, September 1991

This is a story about my little sister and me.

Usually we got along well together. But ... sometimes my little sister was a real pest. Particularly when I had to baby-sit.

But she was a good listener
when I told bedtime stories.

Sometimes I hated
having to share things
with her all the time.

But she was a great pirate!

One day my little sister did a terrible thing.

She thought that my pet turtle needed more exercise.

So she decided to set it free in the pond!

When I saw what she had done, I was madder than I'd ever been before.

I could have killed her right there and then.

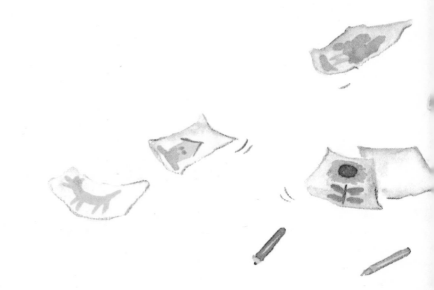

But my parents didn't like that idea
and separated us quickly.

My sister said that she was sorry.
  But I felt that was not enough!
  I was very angry.

She even offered to buy me a new turtle
with her pocket money. But I didn't want a new one.
I wanted MY turtle back!

My parents didn't say much. They seemed to be on her side. I went to my room and slammed the door as loudly as I could.

I thought of many ways to punish my little sister.

I tried to get some sleep.

But it didn't work.

I began to feel sick. I was convinced
I even had a temperature!

I was too upset to get out of bed. Meanwhile, my sister was singing and dancing in the garden. She seemed to be having the best time of her life.

I was the one who was upset and my little sister didn't seem to care at all. My turtle was gone! How could she forget all about it so easily. I was mad, mad, MAD!

I punched my pillows
a few times as hard as I could,
let go of an awful scream...

and felt a lot better.

Finally I knew what to do.

I got up and put on my shoes.

Then I went outside to where my sister was feeding the dog.

I said to her, "I'll help you with that," and she smiled.

"By the way," I said after a little while, "the thing with the turtle is OK. I'm not angry anymore."

"Does that mean we are friends again?" asked my sister.

"Yes," I said. "We're friends again."

I was surprised how easy it was to say that. Then I asked her, "Do you want to come to the pet shop with me?"

"To buy a new turtle?"

"No," I said and smiled.

"We are going to buy a couple of hamsters,"
I said. "One for you and one for me. We can
keep them in the old aquarium."

My sister took my hand and off we went.